THE
LOTTERY

BY HELEN KAULBACH

The Lottery
Copyright © 2016 Helen Kaulbach

ISBN: 13: 1541326849

Electronic Version published - Amazon Kindle
Print Version published: Createspace

Author: Helen Kaulbach
E-mail: **kaulbach45@gmail.com**

Cover design by Helen Kaulbach.

Clipart by Shutterstock.

Dedicated to Kacey and Kailyn, my two lovely granddaughters, with the hope that someday I will win a lottery and share some of it with them.

Many thanks to my daughter, Kristal Kaulbach, and her colleague, Julie Backer, for their proofreading and editing expertise.

Sometimes life brings you joy,
And sometimes it brings sorrow.
Sometimes life is boringly mundane,
And sometimes it throws you a curve that leaves you gasping.
Sometimes you help someone,
And in the process are helped yourself.
Sometimes life gives you a lemon,
And it's up to you whether you suck it straight or make lemonade.
Sometimes you take a step in a different direction,
And your life is changed forever.
Sometimes your life is calm and serene,
And that's when fate trips you, sending you sprawling in the dust.
Sometimes life just goes on and on
And nobody really notices.
Sometimes life is so good it's almost perfect,
And that's when you get really scared.

Table of Contents

Prologue

Elly Carter made her way slowly through the mall. She was wearing a bright red slicker over her pant suit.

Her arthritis was especially painful today. Her knee and hip had been aching all morning, and now throbbed painfully as she walked on the mall's hard tile floor. But walk she would. She didn't want to end up like Old Grumpy, Mr. Grumman, who lived one floor up from her apartment in Seniors' Haven.

Old Grumpy, as most of the other residents called him, also had arthritis. One day, about a year ago, he sat in one of the wheelchairs usually left in the front lobby for the residents' use, and was still in the wheelchair. In a classic case of "use it or lose it", Old Grumpy could no longer walk and the wheelchair was now his life.

Walking the mall was Elly's favorite Thursday morning activity. The seniors' apartment building was three blocks from the mall. On a good day she walked it. Today it was snowing so she'd taken the bus.

Thursday was lottery ticket day for Elly. She always had a ticket in the Wednesday evening draw. Every Thursday morning she checked her ticket to see if she'd won and bought another ticket for next week.

She had a little ritual, a system of rewards. If she won $2.00 she treated herself to a coffee and cinnamon roll in the food court. If she won $10.00, a rare occurrence, she splurged and spent half of it on a bowl of soup and a pot of tea in the small tearoom tucked into one corner of the mall.

She didn't know what she'd do if she won more. It had never happened. Most Thursdays she won nothing. Those days she sat at a table in the food court sipping on a bottle of water brought from home, and enjoying a small treat she'd saved just for this trip. Sometimes a square or half a muffin; sometimes just an Oreo cookie.

What she ate really wasn't important. What Elly liked was people watching. She could sit in the mall for hours watching the people go by. She liked to make up little stories about interesting people she saw. She never knew if she was right or wrong, as most of the people she never saw again. It fascinated her that these were people with lives elsewhere, jobs, families, children, and even grandchildren. A whole existence that she knew nothing about; just as they knew nothing about her. They could be princes, they could be murderers, but most likely they were merely ordinary people.

They just happened to come within ten feet of each other on a Thursday morning at the mall.

Elly approached the lottery booth with her ticket in hand. The girl behind the counter this morning was Susan, the friendly one. She always had a smile and a hello for her, shook her head when Elly had a losing ticket and rejoiced with her when she won something.

Without even waiting for Elly to ask, Susan punched the lottery machine and ran a printout of last night's winning numbers. She knew Elly liked to sit down and check her numbers slowly, knew she wasn't going to check them while still in front of the lottery booth.

Elly sat on a bench near the lottery booth and watched Susan work. She laughed and talked to every customer as if they were her best friends. But Elly knew better. Susan had few friends. One day when Susan was on break and sipping a cola on the bench, Elly sat down and said hello.

After months of selling her lottery tickets and socializing on the mall bench, Susan opened up and told her story. She'd been an abused wife who'd taken her baby daughter and fled her home in another city. Now living a thousand miles from her ex-husband, she was working two jobs to make a home for her daughter. And as much as she trusted Elly, she'd never told her the name of the city where she used to live.

One of Elly's fantasies, as she people-watched in the mall, was a happy ending for Susan.

Elly limped slowly along to her favorite place in the mall. Just outside the drug store was a grouping of big, upholstered easy chairs, put there by the mall management for the seniors to wait in comfort while they had their prescriptions filled. After school those chairs would be taken over by loud teens, talking on cell phones and eyeing the opposite sex. But on a Thursday morning, there was usually an empty chair to be found.

She took off the red slicker, folded it in her lap, sank into the chair and pulled a pencil from her purse. Propping her lottery ticket on her purse, she started checking her numbers.

She had the first number, and carefully circled it.

Then the second, third and fourth. With each number she circled, her eyes got wider and her pencil slowed.

When she circled the fifth number, the pencil lead broke from the pressure.

She checked the sixth number, and she had that one too.

She stared at the five circled numbers and the sixth one that also matched, disbelief on her face. Checking the others sitting near her, she saw no one she knew. None of the regulars, only strangers. There was no one she could share her good fortune with. But that didn't matter. She was used to enjoying herself on her own.

Elly tucked her winning ticket into her purse and got up painfully from the low chair. Today she would go to the food court and have lunch. She would eat whatever she wanted, because she would soon be rich.

Chapter 1

12:00 noon

Elly circled the food court and decided on her lunch. The Chinese food looked good. She ordered deep-fried shrimp, stir-fried vegetables and rice. The young girl serving behind the counter looked harried although it was still early and most of the lunch crowd hadn't arrived yet. She glanced furtively over her shoulder at the kitchen in behind, and didn't pay much attention to what she was doing, giving Elly a huge portion of shrimp – much more than she could eat. She pointed this out to the girl, who looked up in fright, panic clear in her almond-shaped eyes. The girl didn't acknowledge the complaint, just pushed the plate across the counter, grabbed the money from Elly's hand, made change and turned to the next customer.

Elly picked up her plate and found a table where she could watch the Chinese girl. This was what she loved. Something was going on and it would be interesting to watch and see if she could guess what it was. She took half of her large order of shrimp, wrapped it in a paper napkin and put it in her purse. They would make a good snack when she got back home. Maybe she'd even share them with Old Grumpy.

Half an hour later she was back in her favorite chair in front of the drug store. The lottery ticket was in her purse, which was clenched tightly in her lap. Her red slicker was tossed over the arm of the huge chair. She was ready for her favorite pastime –people watching.

Mei-Li

"You no good girl. You very slow. Hurry! Hurry!" In the tiny cramped kitchen of the Chinese restaurant in the food court, the manager, Chang, was on his usual morning rampage. Mei-Li was transferring the cooked food from the woks on the gas burners to the containers out front where the customers could see them. It was still too early for the main lunch customers, but already people were wandering past, looking at the food selection and checking the menu boards.

Mei-Li had been there since early this morning, helping to chop and slice the mounds of vegetables used in all the different dishes and stirring the rice until it was the "right" consistency. She'd had only one 10-minute break all morning, during which she managed to eat a bowl of rice and share a pot of tea with Lee, the cook. She looked longingly at the cooked chicken and pork, but knew that Chang would never let her touch them. On the rare occasion when Chang left the kitchen, Lee sometimes passed her a couple of pieces of meat in a napkin. She ate them with her fingers and disposed of the napkin outside, so there would be no trace for Chang to see. She felt guilty for going behind Chang's back, but reasoned she needed the protein to give her the energy to get through her long day.

And it was a long day. She spent all morning working in the kitchen, then served at the counter during the lunch hour. She got two hours off in the middle of the afternoon and then was back in time to help prepare for the dinner crowd. Then after serving at the counter for dinner, she and Lee had to wash all the cooking pots and clean the kitchen before they could leave. By the time she left for the day, she had put in twelve hours and was exhausted.

She knew that working those long hours every day was against the law, but she couldn't complain. She'd come to Canada on the understanding that she would work to pay off her expenses in getting here and be able to send money back to her family so they could also come some day. She couldn't let them down.

In a lull between customers, Mei-Li closed her eyes for a moment and thought about her family. So far she hadn't been able to send them anything. Her payback on her traveling expenses and her rent on her tiny room used up all her wages.

Also Chang was always threatening to hold back more of her wages if she didn't work faster. Just yesterday she had burned her hand on a hot wok and had to take fifteen minutes to get it bandaged. Chang made her work one of her two free hours, at no pay, to make up for it.

"You no good girl. No standing doing nothing. Work! Work, or I no pay you for this hour." Mei-Li, startled at Chang coming up behind her, looked frantically around. There were no customers waiting and all the trays were filled with food. Trying to look busy, she went over and stirred the rice. An elderly lady in a red coat, who she remembered seeing there before, ordered a combo meal. Rattled by her encounter with Chang, she put two scoops of shrimp on the plate instead of one. The lady pointed this out, but Mei-Li, glancing around to make sure Chang was nowhere to be seen, shook her head and passed her the overfilled plate. Let someone benefit from Chang's meanness, she thought.

As she worked the lunch hour she kept thinking about the card in her pocket. Another girl, Miko, who used to live in the room next to hers but had moved out a couple of months ago, had come by the food court yesterday and walked around the mall with her during her free time.

Miko was well dressed, although a bit flashy for Mei-Li's taste, and kept talking about her new job for what she called an "escort service." She was making a lot of money, had her own apartment and was able to send money back home to China to her family. She urged Mei-Li to join her.

"You'll never earn enough money working in that restaurant," she said. "You'll be in debt for years and your family will be too old to come."

Mei-Li was no fool. She knew that the escort service was just another name for prostitution. But the money was tempting. *I can always do it for just a couple of years,* she thought, *and find a decent job before my family comes.* Miko gave her a business card and said she could call any time and someone would come and pick her up. Or she could just come to the office on her own and talk to the other girls. No one would pressure her.

When Mei-Li left the food court on her afternoon break, she spotted the elderly lady in the red coat sitting in one of the chairs outside the drug store. She looked so happy and contented with her life that Mei-Li felt a sharp pang of envy. She wanted to be that happy as she grew old, and she knew that, for her, happiness meant having her family near. In that instant she made up her mind. She would not go back to the restaurant that evening. She would go downtown and find the address on the card.

She left the mall and started walking, excited and a little scared, but looking hopefully ahead to her new life.

Chapter 2

12:30 pm

Early afternoon was a good time for people-watching. Seated in her comfortable chair, Elly could see mainly two types of people. There were the business girls shopping on their lunch hour; well-dressed, tense, with a definite destination in mind. Browsing was not for them.

Then there were the ones Elly loved best: the mothers with small children. They walked slowly and casually through the mall, pushing their strollers with one or two children. Sometimes the strollers held two and a third walked alongside, hurrying on short stubby legs to keep up with mother. These were not shoppers. They were just there for the exercise. On a cold or wet day, the mall was filled with mothers and babies.

Always on the alert for someone a little different, Elly's eye was caught by someone who fit both scenarios, but not quite. She was pushing a stroller with a toddler in it and a boy, about four, walked along beside her. But instead of the jeans and sweatshirts most of the other mothers wore, this one was smartly dressed in tailored pants and blazer. The four-year-old was working his way through an ice cream cone while the mother fed small spoonfuls to the toddler from her own cone.

She stopped near Elly's chair to wipe the smaller child's face with a napkin. Seeing Elly smiling at her and the children, she smiled back.

Marcia

Marcia hummed to herself as she fed her two children an early lunch. She planned to arrive at the mall before noon and get some of her shopping done before it got busy in the afternoon.

She loved this new work schedule her department at the Municipal Library had worked out with management. It was called the "Nine-Day Fortnight," and by working 50 minutes extra for nine days, they were able to take one whole day off every second week. That gave her an extra day to do things around the house and spend some quality time with Liam and Becka. Her youngest, would celebrate her first birthday on Christmas Day. Her full name was Rebekah but Liam found it too difficult to pronounce and could only manage Becka. The name stuck and now everyone called her that.

Marcia already had most of her Christmas shopping done. Gifts for her parents, her sister and her sister's children were piled on the dining room table waiting to be mailed. Jack's gifts were hidden in the laundry room, a place he went as seldom as possible, and the kids' gifts were on the top shelf in her bedroom closet. She even had some Christmas baking tucked away in the freezer.

The washer had stopped as she was dressing Becka and she had taken a moment to toss the clothes in the dryer before replacing Liam's shoes on the right feet and going out the door.

Lunch was in full swing as they passed the food court in the mall. So far it had been a good shopping trip; there were already three parcels in the basket under Becka's stroller seat.

"Mommy," Liam said, tugging on her sleeve. "You promised us an ice cream for dessert."

"I did. But not in the food court. It's too busy. There's another ice cream place down by Sears. We'll get it there."

"I want strawberry today."

Marcia smiled. Liam always had strawberry ice cream. Sometimes he asked her to read the flavors, and took a long time considering, but he always came back to strawberry. Other times, like today, he thought about it before arriving at the ice cream counter and announced his decision as if he changed flavors often.

"Strawberry it is then. I think Becka and I will have peach yogurt."

"Does Becka get her own today?"

"Not in the mall, she doesn't. Too messy. She and I will share."

A few minutes later they stopped for their cones and Marcia asked for one of their small tasting spoons to feed Becka.

The next stop was at the drug store, but Marcia was reluctant to go in the store while they still had ice cream. So they slowed down and looked at some teddy bears in a store window. When the ice cream cones were almost gone, she stopped near a bank of chairs with a trash can nearby and used napkins to clean up the children.

An elderly lady was sitting in one of the chairs, with a red coat tossed across the chair arm. She smiled at Becka and got a big grin in return.

"Lovely children," she said to Marcia. "Children are a blessing, especially at Christmas."

"Thank you. And yes, they are a blessing. Even when they're sticky with ice cream."

They shared a laugh before Marcia pushed the stroller into the drug store.

Half an hour later she was back outside the mall, buckling Liam and Becka into their booster seats in the back seat of the car.

At the parking lot exit she had to stop for a minute while three fire trucks roared by. Liam bounced around in his seat, imitating the sirens.

Marcia smiled back at him. What was it about little boys that they loved fire trucks and police cars?

"Look at them suckers go," yelled Liam.

"Liam," admonished his mother. "That's not a nice word."

"Well, that's what Jason said at school the other day when the fire trucks went by. And Teacher didn't say anything."

Turning off the highway on her way home, she noticed smoke spiraling up in the distance and wondered if the fire was anywhere near their street.

She was thinking about dinner tonight and the new recipe she'd found for chicken breasts. She was about to turn into her street before she noticed the fire engines and the police car blocking the intersection.

Looking down the street, past the fire engines, she saw with horror that it was her house on fire. And not just a little smoke, but flame roaring out every window and through the roof. She slammed on the brakes just in time before hitting the police car and leaped from her car.

She started to run down the street but the policeman caught her by the arm.

"Sorry Ma'am. You can't go in there now."

"But…but, that's my house. I have to go."

The policeman became instantly alert. "The first thing we need to know, Ma'am, is if there was anyone in the house."

Marcia stared at him for a moment, her mind a blank. Then she understood what he wanted.

"No, there was no one else at home."

He spoke briefly into his radio and then walked Marcia back to her car.

"Perhaps you'd like to park your car against the curb, out of the intersection. If you don't feel up to it, I can move it for you."

"No. No, I can do it."

"Then I'll go get the Fire Chief. I think he wants to talk to you."

She opened the car door and saw a look of such fear and horror on Liam's face that she knew why the policeman wanted her to move her car. From his vantage point on a booster seat by the window Liam had a direct view of their house burning. She needed to get it out of his line of sight immediately. Thankfully, Becka was sound asleep in her seat and hadn't seen anything.

After she moved her car, she took out her cell phone to call her husband at work. She was standing in the intersection, mesmerized by the flames, when one whole section of roof fell in with a roar, sending sparks and heavy smoke skyward.

That was when it struck her. *It's all gone. All my Christmas presents, all my clothes, all my jewelry, everything I own. Everything Jack owns. His new golf clubs, his prized wooden carvings that were all he had left of his father. Even our wedding pictures. The children's toys and Becka's favorite blanket. They're all gone.*

The tears slipped down her cheeks as she turned and walked back to her car.

She was standing there with the car door open when a firefighter walked up with a notebook and started asking questions. The first; was she positive there was no one else in the house?

"No, no one else at home."

"Any pets?"

"No."

"Would you have left a pot on the stove? Candles burning? Any appliances on?"

"Just the dryer. I put in a load just before I left."

"That could be it. Those suckers get pretty hot. Especially when lint builds up in the vent pipe." Liam looked up at the sound of the word he wasn't supposed to say, looking with his haunted face from his mother to the fireman.

"I think you should know, ma'am," said the fireman hesitantly, "that we were here in less than four minutes after the alarm was called in. But the structure was fully involved when we arrived. With no one home on either side of you or across the street, there was a definite delay in reporting the fire. At that point there was little we could do to salvage your house, so we concentrated on keeping it from spreading. I'm sorry. I know it's hard, coming just before Christmas and all."

Needing to connect with something that was still hers, she sat on the edge of the back seat and put her arms around Liam. So far he hadn't said a word since realizing it was his house on fire. Now his little chest heaved and great wracking sobs stuttered out. When Jack arrived a few minutes later he found mother and son with their arms wrapped around each other, sobbing as if their hearts would break. With his own near to breaking too, he joined them.

Chapter 3

1:00 pm

Elly hated to leave her big comfortable armchair in front of the drug store, but nature was calling. That second cup of tea with lunch was making her uncomfortable.

She debated whether to leave her red slicker on the chair to hold it, but was afraid someone would steal it while she was gone. Although she was now rich enough to afford to buy herself a new coat, she didn't actually have any money yet. And she needed the coat to wear home later. So she picked up her coat and purse and headed toward the restroom.

Averil

Averil pulled into the mall parking lot and found an empty spot in front of the drug store. It was ironic that today, when she could have used the extra walk, she should find a parking spot so close.

She was excited, but apprehensive. Desperate to know for sure if she was really pregnant, but fearful of being disappointed yet again. After four years of trying, she and Chet were afraid it would never happen. But now it looked as if they might have gotten lucky.

She had been so busy these past few weeks helping plan her sister's wedding and acting as her Matron of Honor, that she'd paid no attention to her own body rhythms. This morning at the office, while checking her calendar, she realized she was almost two weeks late.

At first she was paralyzed with shock. Then elation set in. This could be it. She did very little work for the rest of the morning, sitting there staring out her office window with a silly grin on her face. She thought of calling Chet and telling him, but decided against it. Better to find out for sure than disappoint him yet again.

On her lunch hour, she'd go to the drug store for one of those home pregnancy kits. Then she'd hurry home after work and do the test before Chet got home.

She sat in the car for a moment before going in; knowing that the results of the test could change her life forever. Now that the moment was here, she wasn't sure she wanted to know. Maybe she should let it ride for another couple of weeks. She'd been late before. Maybe this was just another false alarm.

Before she could change her mind she went into the drug store and purchased the kit.

She was about to put the kit in her handbag and return to her car when she realized she had to go to the bathroom, so walked through the store and out into the mall. In the mall restroom she made a decision. Now that she had the kit, she was so anxious to know the result that she couldn't wait to go home. So she stood there in the washroom stall carefully reading the directions, and just as carefully followed them. She was there a long time; several people came and went as she held the stick waiting for it to change color.

When she saw the first faint tinge of color her heart gave a leap. As the color darkened the grin that had been there most of the morning got even wider.

"Yes," she yelled, punching the air with her fist. "We finally did it."

Averil opened the door and came out, a little embarrassed at seeing Elly standing there staring at her, but so happy she didn't care.

"I'm pregnant," she said, beaming at Elly. When Elly, smiling back, touched her on the shoulder, she grabbed the older woman, lifted her off her feet and swung her around. "I'm sorry," she said, abashed at her behavior. "But I'm just so happy. We've waited a long time for this, Chet and I. We're finally going to be parents.'"

"And I'm happy for you," said Elly, staggering a little as her arthritic knees fought to keep her balance when Averil released her.

Elly walked back into the mall with the smile still on her face, and was happy to see that her favourite chair was still unoccupied.

Chapter 4

1:30 pm

A couple, just barely past retirement age were walking through the mall, holding hands. The man looking at his wife so adoringly that just looking at them made Elly feel as if she were trespassing. There goes a couple with a marvelous retirement ahead of them, she mused. They are so lucky to have each other.

She shifted a bit in her chair to get more comfortable and her red coat fell on the floor. The man stopped to pick it up, shook it, folded it and passed it back to her. "That's too pretty a coat to get dirty on this floor," he said. "Have a good day."

What a nice man, thought Elly. I hope she realizes he's a keeper.

Bert & Sharon

"You don't really have to come with me you know," Sharon said as they strolled through the mall. "I'm a big girl. I can take it."

"Maybe you can…. take it that is, but you shouldn't have to. Not alone, and especially if the news is bad." He took her hand and patted it. "I wasn't there when the doctor first told you that you had a problem. But I was there when they did the biopsy. And I'm going to be there when they tell you the results. We're a team, you know. After all these years, surely you can't forget that."

She gave him a sad little smile. "All I've ever wanted to be was on your team. And we were the best, you know, all those years. Now that we're finally retired, I was hoping we could stay teammates in another way. Go places, do things together."

"We'll still do them. If not this year, then next. We're still young and we've got a lot of retirement years ahead of us."

They went into the drug store where Bert made a few purchases, shaving cream and hair goop. Sharon wandered around, picking up things and putting them down again. She wasn't really interested in anything, with the doctor's visit filling her thoughts. She had a feeling she knew what the result would be, and she was sure Bert did too. But until they actually knew, they were both keeping up appearances for the other.

Leaving the drug store, Sharon's eye was caught by a splotch of bright red in one of the armchairs the store put in the mall for the use of its customers. A tiny gray-haired lady with her red coat tossed over the arm of the chair, and guarding her purse fiercely, was looking interestedly around at the other shoppers. She moved in her chair and her coat fell on the floor. Bert stopped and picked it up for her. She briefly caught Sharon's eye and smiled.

Sharon smiled back, momentarily forgetting her problems. Then the thought struck her that the lady with the red coat was probably 20 years older than herself. She wondered, with a pang, if she would still be around at that age.

The doctor's office was utilitarian, like most waiting rooms. Hard chairs, outdated magazines and an atmosphere of tension and unease. The only bright spot was a tropical fish tank in one corner.

When her name was called, Sharon's heart started to pound. Bert just sat there unmoving, so she grabbed his hand and pulled.

"You wanted to come, so don't cop out on me now."

Bert reluctantly got to his feet and followed her. They were led, not to an examining room, but to the doctor's private office. Sharon noted this and felt even more apprehensive. Dr. Milano smiled as he waved them to the chairs.

They were barely settled when he looked up from the file on his desk, and this time there was no smile.

"We won't waste time with small talk because I know you're anxious to hear the results of the biopsy." When they nodded in unison, he went on. "You've known from the beginning that there was a significant chance that this was cancer. And, I'm sorry to have to tell you that that's what we found." He paused a moment to let that fact sink in.

Sharon's face lost all color as she looked at Bert. She'd known that was what she was going to hear, but it still hit hard to have it in words. Bert picked up her hand and squeezed it, then turned to Dr. Milano.

"So, what's next? How do we fight this?"

"From what we can tell so far, it looks to be in the early stages, We won't know for certain until after surgery, but there's an excellent chance for a good outcome."

"Surgery?" Sharon picked up on that one word.

"If you were younger, I might recommend a lumpectomy, followed by radiation and chemo. However, at your age, my recommendation would be a modified radical mastectomy. If we get it all and there is no lymph node involvement, then we don't have to put you through the trauma of chemo. We will still be removing and checking some lymph nodes, and if we find any involvement, then further treatment will be necessary. But we'll cross that bridge when we come to it."

"I'm stunned," said Sharon. "We just retired. We had so many plans. I wasn't expecting to face something like this right now." She took out a tissue and wiped her eyes.

"No one expects this, at any time," said Dr. Milano kindly. "But we have to look at this positively. First, I think we've caught this early enough. Secondly, with surgery you'll have your life back on track in a few months. Even if you require further treatment it'll be, at most, a year. Consider this a bump in the road, a slight delay in your retirement plans. At least there are two of you. I have so many patients who have to go through this alone. You're luckier than some." He nodded at their tightly clenched hands and smiled.

"Now for the details.... I'd like to schedule surgery as soon as possible. The sooner we do it, the sooner you can get on with your life."

Chapter 5

2:00 pm

Elly settled herself deeper into her chair, feeling a little drowsy. The lunchtime crowd in business suits and tailored dresses was starting to thin out. For the next hour the mall would be filled with seniors. They usually waited until after lunch when the mall was not so busy. They tended to avoid the mornings when the mall was filled with young mothers and babies in strollers. And tried to finish their errands and leave the mall before the after-school influx of boisterous teenagers.

Elly didn't mind the teens. She'd gotten to know the regulars and some of them had even started saying hello to her. They enjoyed the deep comfortable chairs around the mall, sometimes sitting four or five to a chair, two wedged into the seat as well as others perched on the arms and back. They were careful not to invade her space, and were, she sensed, better behaved when she was around. The teens often hurled foul language, including the F-word, at each other as they walked by in the mall. But they seldom, if ever, used it while sitting next to her.

A well-dressed man in his forties came out of the drug store with a small bag in his hand. She'd seen him before and thought he worked in one of the office buildings attached to the mall. He stopped by the trash can, removed a small bottle from the bag and put it in his pocket, tossing the bag in the trash. Seeing Elly watching him, he gave her a small smile and started whistling as he walked off toward the office tower.

Marc

Marc sat at his desk in the brokerage office in the office building attached to the mall. It was only 10 am, but he'd been at his desk since before eight writing out an elaborate scheme to fix something he had done a couple of weeks ago.

About a month ago, his live-in girlfriend, Elana, had left him in the middle of the day, taking everything she could cram into her car, including all his computers and electronics, and had cleaned out their joint household bank account. He had just deposited the funds for that month the day before. Any attempt to find her came up blank. In the next week he had to pay his mortgage, credit card balance, all the utilities and replace the computers and electronic equipment that he needed. Elana had been high-maintenance to start with and he had mostly drained his savings providing her with the designer clothes and jewelry she loved.

Strapped for cash and a pile of bills to pay, he did something he now realized was incredibly foolish. He created a new brokerage account in a fictitious name and "borrowed" funds from one of his elderly clients whose account he had authority to manage. This morning, realizing he could never cover it just with his regular commissions, he was going to see his banker and remortgage his house. It was an expensive lesson but he had to do it before the auditors noticed the missing funds.

He spent an embarrassing hour with his banker, reluctant at first to admit how he'd let Elana dupe him. He did not mention the dummy brokerage account, only his need for money to pay debts. He got the new mortgage, signed all the papers and then decided to have lunch before heading back to the office.

By this time he had a pounding headache and stopped by the drugstore to pick up a bottle of Tylenol. Outside the drugstore a red coat caught his eye and he spotted a lady he had seen before in the mall. She was sitting in one of the comfortable chairs surrounded by a few other seniors. As he had often seen her sitting there, he gave her a smile as he went by.

He was pleased with himself as he went back to the office, relieved that he now had the funds to get himself out of what could be a nasty situation.

His happy feeling disappeared when he entered his office to find his boss sitting behind his desk flanked by two men from security.

"What's going on?" he asked.

Standing up, but still staying behind the desk, his boss asked, "You didn't think you'd get away with it did you? An interim audit yesterday turned up an irregularity and we had someone working on it all morning."

"But...but...I've got it covered." stammered Marc.

"Sorry, Marc, but you'll have to tell that to the judge. You're being charged with fraud and I suggest you get a lawyer. These guys," he indicated the security officers, "are here to see you clear out your personal items from your desk, leaving your client files behind, and they will escort you from the building."

Chapter 6

2:30 pm

Elly thought about Susan, the lottery ticket seller, as she sat in her chair in front of the drug store. Now that she had money she could do something to help her. She knew the lottery ticket booth would get a royalty for selling the winning ticket, but knew also that the money would go to the company that held the concession. She doubted that Susan would see any of it.

Perhaps she would buy Susan a house. Not a large one, just a little bungalow where her daughter could have a room of her own and a yard to play in. It would be far better for her than that one-bedroom apartment she had in a rough part of town.

Five million dollars was a lot of money and a 75-year-old lady didn't need that much to live. She could do a lot of good with some of that money and still have enough to live in comfort the rest of her life

Yes, she thought, I'll buy Susan a little house. She'll protest, but I'll point out how much better it will be for her daughter. Then perhaps I'll write a will and leave her some money as well. She deserves a better life than she has.

She smiled to herself at the irony of making life-changing plans for someone she didn't know very well and paying for it with money she still didn't have.

She came out of her reverie as two other mall regulars waved to her as they passed by.

Barney and Patricia spent most cold, rainy days in the mall. They were always together. Elly never saw one without the other and felt happy for them that they had each other. They were both disabled and both used power wheelchairs to get around.

Barney and Patricia

Barney arrived at the mall before Patricia today. He had something special to do. He went straight to the jewelry store he had checked out a few days ago. A clerk, who had seen Barney in the store before, came out from behind the counter and held the door open while Barney maneuvered his powered wheelchair into the store.

He spent a couple of minutes explaining to the clerk what he wanted and how much he could afford to pay.

"Not a ring," he said, "because her knuckles are quite swollen and her fingers a bit crooked. She's quite self-conscious of them. I think a pendant would be best."

The clerk brought out a tray of gold and diamond pendants and Barney chose three. He liked the gold heart with the single diamond in the center, but wasn't sure which Patricia would like, so he'd give her a choice within his price range. He asked the clerk to put those three aside and said he and Patricia would be in later.

A few minutes later he met Patricia in their usual spot outside the food court.

"Hey Barn," she called from where she'd been checking out a store window. "You're late today. I was going to go grab us a table before they're all gone."

"I'm glad you didn't. I'm taking you to La Brioche for lunch today to celebrate your birthday."

"But my birthday's not 'til next week."

"So what! Maybe I'll be broke next week. We'll go today."

Patricia smiled fondly at him and reversed her wheelchair away from the window. They made their way slowly to the restaurant at the other end of the mall. Partway there she signaled him to stop.

"You know I have trouble handling a knife and cutting up meat, don't you?"

"So we'll have fish and chips that you can eat with your fingers."

She laughed and they trundled off down the mall, the small red flags fastened to the backs of the chairs bobbing in unison.

In the restaurant Patricia opted for the chicken fingers, explaining it was still finger food but not quite as greasy as the fish.

When they finished and Barney suggested dessert, Patricia gave him a hard stare.

"You've got something on your mind, haven't you? Are you moving again?" Her voice rose slightly. "That's it, isn't it? You're moving again and you don't want to tell me."

Barney reached across and held her hand, rubbing the swollen knuckles.

"No, I'm not moving. But I'd like to if I could move in with you." He cleared his throat nervously. "Patricia, do you think it's possible we could move in together? I've been thinking a lot about us lately, and I'd really like us to get married."

"Married? Barney, could we really? I know we love each other, but we live in different group homes, and we both need part time personal care help. Do you think it's possible?"

"I think it's very possible. I was planning to ask you on your birthday, but something's come up. A vacancy has opened up in the home where I live and I asked them about you. They're all for it. The room is next to mine and they'll even put in a connecting door for us so we can have our own private suite."

Patricia's face glowed with happiness as she watched Barney paying their bill and maneuvering his chair away from the table. She loved this man but never really thought they could have a home together.

"Let's go," he said leading the way out of the restaurant. "Now that we're engaged, let's go buy a diamond to make it official."

Chapter 7

3:00 pm

Elly sighed as she watched the two boys walking into the mall through the outside doors. Although "walking" wasn't exactly what they were doing. They were running, shoving each other, darting from side to side and using their backpacks to pummel each other. School had just let out and they were in high spirits. She knew they were headed for the big soft chairs and would pile into them, pushing and shoving and talking at high volume, as they waited for their friends to appear. Sometimes they took over all the chairs and she was forced to go somewhere else when their antics became unbearable. Today only one was unoccupied so she hoped they wouldn't stay. The third chair in their grouping was occupied by a clerk from one of the dress shops who had taken off her shoes and was enjoying a coffee break. She glared at the boys, who instinctively knew better than to bother her. A bench situated just outside the grouping of easy chairs held three older men, closer to Elly's age. They were discussing s hockey game they'd seen on TV the evening before.

The two teens flopped into the one empty chair and immediately took out their cell phones and started texting to friends elsewhere in the mall, coordinating where they would meet.

Walter

Walter pulled into the last remaining handicapped parking spot near the drugstore. He felt a little guilty, but also a little defiant. The handicap tag on his car had belonged to his late wife, and two years later he still hadn't returned it. He told himself that his knees were bothering him, he was getting older, and he really needed it. His slow movements as he got out of the car and walked into the store would have vindicated him if anyone were watching.

He walked into the drugstore with his prescription in his hand. It seemed like every month he had something else wrong with him, and each time he went to the doctor he came away with a new prescription. As far as he was concerned, the only thing wrong with him was loneliness. He missed Miriam and he missed her cooking. He could sure use a good home cooked meal. But what did these young doctors know? All they knew was running tests and writing prescriptions. What did they know about loneliness?

Perhaps when he finished in the drugstore he would sit by that lady he'd often seen here before; Elly, he thought her name was. Maybe she was lonely too and would enjoy someone to talk to.

Coming out of the drugstore, Walter started across to the chairs, heading for the one next to Elly. Before he got there two teens ran past him, jumped into the last empty chair and took out their cell phones.

Walter stood for a moment, unsure what to do and then he got angry. He started to say something, but nothing came out and he started to fall.

Elly and the others watched in horror as Walter crumpled to the floor and just lay there. One of the men got up to go over to him and Elly said to one of the boys who had stopped texting to look, "Call 911." The boy just stared at her and then at Walter on the floor, eyes wide in fear. Elly reached over and swatted the boy on the arm and yelled, "Just do it! Call 911 like I told you."

The frightened boy did as he was told.

Minutes later the area in front of the drugstore was full of paramedics, mall security, shoppers stopping to see what was going on and horrified seniors who knew that what happened to Walter could just as easily have happened to them.

The two boys were nowhere in sight.

Chapter 8

3:30 pm

Elly, shaken by Walter's collapse and the turmoil of security and ambulances, got up from her chair and thought she would walk for a while. She remembered that her grandson had a birthday coming up so went to the card shop to buy him a card. Usually she bought her greeting cards at the dollar store, but with a winning lottery ticket tucked into her purse, she thought she would buy him a nice card for a change, maybe even slip some money into the envelop as a surprise.

It occurred to her that she could also help her grandkids with her new windfall. Two of them were in their last year of high school and could probably use some help for college costs. Her oldest granddaughter, married only a year and already expecting her first child, she was positive could use some help. Having a great-grandchild was going to be an interesting experience. The start of a whole new generation she would enjoy spoiling.

She took a while choosing the card and then headed off to the Post Office for a stamp.

Devi

Devi hurried along the mall toward Form Fit Fashions where she worked every afternoon after school. Working every day meant she had no after-school social life, but that didn't matter. She had plans. Big plans. She entered the store, calling out hello to Henny the store manager as she made her way to the staff room in back to change into her work clothes. Form Fit Fashions sold high-end leisure and work-out clothes, and when Devi first got the job her manager suggested that the jeans and t-shirt she wore to school were perhaps not the best clothes for work. When Devi admitted that these were all the clothes she had, and one of the things she intended to do with her earnings at the store was purchase some decent clothes, Henny went in the back and came out with a black jacket, matching pants and a tan logo'd shirt to go with it. It had been a return and luckily was a perfect fit for Devi.

Since then Devi wore the black and tan outfit every day for work. She kept it at the store during the week and changed after school, only taking it home on the weekend to wash it. That way the outfit was never left at home with her mother. Devi knew that her mother, an alcoholic, knowing the value of the black suit, might have sold it to buy booze. Living in a dysfunctional family, with alcohol and drugs a normal part of family life and a father who simply disappeared one day and never showed up again, her job at FFF was the first part of her plan to get out of there.

From a young age she'd used school and studying as a way to block out what was happening at home. Because of this, she'd always gotten good grades and attracted the attention of several of her teachers who encouraged her and steered her toward enrichment classes in the subjects she loved best, science and math. Deep inside, she had a dream, which she'd never mentioned to anyone. She wanted to be a doctor. She had no idea how she was going to do it, but do it she would. She'd certainly had lots of practice bandaging up cuts and bruises when her mother was falling-down drunk, or when she got in a brawl in a bar. Once she'd even splinted a broken arm and walked with her sobbing mother to the hospital emergency because they had no money for the bus.

On her mid-term exams she'd gotten all A's and glowing reports from her teachers. One of her teachers helped her research scholarships and send applications to several universities. So far she hadn't heard from any of them. Not trusting her mother to respect her privacy, she had put the store's address and P.O. box number on all her applications.

Today when Devi came out on the sales floor, the store was almost deserted.

"Why don't you go and get our mail," suggested Henny. "Here's the Post Office box key." Henny knew about the applications and that she was desperate to hear back from them.

Devi hurried along the mall toward the Post Office. When she spotted Elly headed in the same direction she slowed down and walked with her. She knew Elly as one of the regulars who hung out in the mall to socialize and she occasionally saw her in the food court when she went there to eat her sandwich on her dinner break.

"How are you doing today, Elly? Knees still hurt?"

"My knees always hurt when it rains," said Elly, "But somehow today they don't feel too bad."

So far she hadn't told anyone about the lottery ticket. That was news she just wanted to hug to herself a little longer.

While Elly was buying her stamp, Devi walked over to the mail boxes and found the one for FFF. Inserting her key she pulled out several letters and spotted one with her own name and a distinctive return address. She let out a whoop that attracted Elly's attention. Devi left the Post Office and sat on a bench outside. Elly sat next to her and peered at the envelope.

"Is that the one you've been waiting for?" she asked.

"Oh yes, and I'm almost afraid to open it. What if they don't want me? What if they do want me and I can't afford it? Unless I get a scholarship I can't go."

Elly smiled to herself. Devi was someone else she could help with her winnings. This winning the lottery was going to be fun!

"Here, I'll hold the rest of your mail while you open it. You know you're not getting off this bench until you see it."

Devi ripped open the envelope and pulling out several sheets, skimmed them quickly, catching her breath as she did. Finally she reached over and gave Elly a hug and whispered, as if she couldn't believe it enough to say it out loud.

"They want me," she said. "They want me. And what's more they're offering me a full-ride scholarship for four years."

Chapter 9

4:00 pm

Elly was so happy for Devi that it put a lightness back in her step as she made her way back to the comfy chairs outside the drugstore. However, there wasn't an empty chair in sight. School was out and teens from the nearby high school had occupied them all. A good time, she decided, to go to the food court and have a cup of tea and one of those delectable pastries from the bakery. Usually that treat was reserved for a special occasion, but, she thought as she patted her purse, today was a special occasion. Soon she'd be able to afford as many pastries as she wanted.

As she stood there thinking about the tea and pastry, one of the boys, the only name she knew, called out to her. Ethan was usually the quietest of the group and her favorite.

"Hey Elly," he called. "There's only two in this chair. I can kick out Mike and share with you, or you can sit on my lap."

Elly chuckled, imagining herself perched on a lap in the midst of all those chattering and texting boys. "Thanks, Ethan. I think I'll pass. I'm on my way to the Food Court.

Ethan and Mike

Ethan and Mike had been best friends since Kindergarten. They lived two blocks apart in a subdivision and their parents knew each other well. Over the years the two had played many sports together and gotten into trouble together. Their parents were fond of saying that whatever one couldn't think of the other could. They were inseparable in other ways, Ethan giving up summer camp one year to stay home and keep Mike company while his broken leg healed.

Ethan, who turned 16 four months ago, had his driver's license, while Mike still had two months to wait. Today they were the first of their group to get to the mall as Ethan's Mom was working from home for a few days and said he could have her car. Being there first meant they got the best seats right outside the drugstore.

For the next hour they laughed and roughhoused with the other guys, and took time out to text a couple of girls. Finally Mike suggested it was time to go as it was almost rush hour.

Exiting the mall, they couldn't believe how heavy the traffic was. It was also starting to get dark and every car had its lights on. Ethan had never driven in traffic like this, especially after dark, and he was a bit nervous. Finally, the light turned green and he gunned the motor to get across the intersection as fast as he could. Neither of them saw the fully loaded semi, going too fast to stop, that entered the intersection on the last of the yellow light and was still going when it turned red. The crash was horrific. Ethan's Mom's little car was hit broadside, rolling it over several times. The truck swerved and hit another car before careening into the traffic light pole. Within minutes police, ambulances and fire trucks arrived, shutting down the intersection and attempting to re-route traffic around the mess. When emergency crews were able to pry open the crushed little car, they were amazed to find both boys still alive. They were unconscious and badly injured but both were still breathing. After assessing both boys, they called for an Air Ambulance to airlift them to the nearest hospital.

Later that evening after both sets of parents had been called and both Ethan and Mike had undergone emergency surgery, the surgeons met with the boys' parents in a waiting room adjacent to Intensive Care.

"Which of you are Mike's parents?" asked one surgeon. They jumped to their feet immediately, fear showing on their faces.

The surgeon smiled. "Mike is going to be OK. He has a concussion and several broken bones. We've put screws in a couple of the fractures and put a cast on one that wasn't quite so bad. He will need a long recovery time and some rehab. But he's young and eventually will recover nicely."

The other surgeon turned to Ethan's parents, still seated with their hands clasped together. "While Mike sustained several injuries, Ethan had only one, but his is a devastating injury. Two of the vertebrae in his neck were crushed and the damage is not repairable. I'm sorry to inform you that your son is now a quadriplegic, paralyzed from the neck down."

Chapter 10

4:30 pm

Elly was still smiling over Ethan's invitation to sit on his lap as she arrived at the food court. She picked up her tea and a slice of apple strudel and looked for a seat, surprised at how busy it was at this time of day. She spotted an empty seat next to a young woman who was halfway through a hamburger. The woman moved her backpack a few inches to give Elly more room on the bench seat. "Thanks," said Elly, as she settled herself and added milk to her tea. "You look like you're having an early dinner."

"More like a late lunch," said the woman. "I missed a couple of classes at the College last week when my daughter was sick, so had to do a make-up class today .No time for lunch so I was starved when I got here." She went on to explain that she received a card in the mail the day before to pick up a registered letter at the Post Office and came here today to get it before picking up her daughter at the school's After Care program.

"Maddie loves the arts and crafts and dance classes at the After Care program, but she gets upset if I'm not there by five." She said as she stood up to leave. "I hope this registered letter isn't about raising my tuition. I sure don't need that right now."

Elly went back to sipping her tea, thinking about the different lives of women these days compared to when she was a young mother. She didn't remember any of her friends going to school while their own children were in school.

Debby

Debby caught the bus outside the Community College, thankful there was still a seat available. She was hungry as she hadn't had time for lunch and thought she'd pick up something at the food court in the mall before going to the Post Office.

She planned to go there before picking up her daughter from her After Care program at school. There wasn't really time in her day for all she had to do, but the card said this letter had to be signed for.

Her life these days seemed to be one big rush. She was halfway through her second year of a two-year computer skills course at the college. A single mother, desperate to get off welfare and make a decent life for herself and her daughter, she had applied for a computer course through a government-sponsored skills training program.

She was doing well in her classes but her biggest challenge was keyboarding. She'd never taken typing in school and had to start with the basics. She found the repetitious practice incredibly boring and at one point almost gave it up. Her instructor suggested she might do better if she practiced on something that interested her; perhaps writing letters to a distant relative or keeping a diary. That wasn't going to work as, being an only child of parents who had her late in life, she had no relatives that she knew of. Keeping a daily diary would consist of "sleep, eat, go to school, play cards with Maddie". That would be as repetitious as "the lazy brown dog".

Then one evening after putting Maddie to bed, she was indulging in her one form of relaxation, reading a romance novel. She loved to lose herself in the story and imagine that it was she who was having those adventures, and hope that one day she would meet a special man. This particular story didn't have much of a plot and she was thinking how she could do it better. Then it struck her: she could do it better. This is how she would improve her typing skills, by writing a romance novel. She'd finally found something that interested her enough to keep her at the keyboard. Six months later she'd finished a first draft and two revisions of the novel and passed her timed typing test.

She went on line and researched romance publishers. After reading their guidelines and marketing strategies, she chose one and mailed off her manuscript. The company warned that new writers and unsolicited manuscripts would take three months for a response, and about 90% were rejected, but in the case of a rejection they would try to include a critique if possible.

Debby didn't expect her first try to be accepted and was actually looking forward to the critique to see how she did. She'd sent it out six weeks ago, so was looking forward to hearing, one way or the other in January.

Her stop for the mall was coming up so she stopped woolgathering, picked up her backpack and edged toward the door. In the mall she headed for the food court and bought a burger before going to the Post Office.

She wasn't looking forward to opening the letter. The one other time she'd received a registered letter it was a lawyer's letter on behalf of her former boyfriend, declaiming any responsibility for her newborn daughter, citing lack of proof of paternity. She was devastated; not so much at the fact that he wasn't contributing to their daughter financially, but that the letter insinuated that she'd been sleeping around while they'd been spending all their free time together. She knew from that day that she would be better off raising her daughter alone than having a man like that in her life. Her experience with registered letters was not great and she was afraid that this one contained more bad news, like a raise in her tuition fees at the school.

While Debby ate her burger, an elderly woman carrying a red coat and a large purse and balancing a tray with a drink and pastry sat next to her. She scooted over to give her more room and they chatted for a while.

She could put it off no longer, so headed off to the Post Office.

Picking up the letter, she turned it over to look at who it was from and was stunned to see the publisher's name and address. The one she had sent her manuscript to.

She couldn't remember drawing a breath as she walked out and sat on the bench in the mall. Ripping open the envelope, a smile spread across her face as she read:

"Congratulations!"

"We are pleased to offer you a contract to publish your novel, Campus Lovers. Please fill in the information below and read and sign the attached contract then return it to us in the enclosed envelope. When we receive the signed contract, you will be mailed an advance in the amount stated."

Debby glanced at the amount of the advance and almost fell off the bench. It was enough to cover her college expenses for the next year and to give Maddie a Christmas this year she'd never forget.

She was plotting her next romance novel before she even left the mall.

Chapter 11

5:00 pm

Elly was lingering in the food court longer than she should have. The afternoon tea crowd had left and now the early birds were coming in for dinner. She recognized a few of them who were regulars there, mostly seniors who tired of cooking for one and liked to get out for a meal a couple of times a week.

There was a commotion as a younger couple came in. Elly guessed they were in their thirties. The woman was crying and the man was talking to her in low tones. They sat down at the table next to Elly. The woman took out a wad of tissues to wipe her face and blow her nose, trying hard to control her sobs and almost succeeding. The man was saying how much he'd like to help her if she would let him.

Elly tried to ignore them, thinking it was a lovers' quarrel until she caught a bit of conversation and realized the two were not lovers as they didn't even know each other's names. She seldom interacted with people she didn't know or who weren't regulars at the mall, but somehow she thought these two needed help.

She reached out and touched the woman's arm to get her attention and said gently, "He really sounds like he wants to help you. Why don't you hear him out?"

The woman stared at her for a moment, then nodded and turned to the man. "I'm sorry. You are being incredibly nice. And it really is all my fault."

Marianne

Marianne left work a little early and headed for the mall. She was hoping that a little retail therapy would boost her out of her blue mood. Here it was almost Christmas and she hadn't even started her Christmas shopping. Nothing seemed to interest her these days.

Three months ago she'd received a promotion to her dream job. The new job came with a transfer to another city, which suited her just fine at the time, as she had recently ended a two year relationship. The trauma of the breakup was still fresh and a new start in a new city sounded wonderful.

She loved her new job and loved going to work, but was totally unprepared for the crushing loneliness of living in a new city where she knew no one. Most of her new colleagues at work were married or in a relationship and they socialized together as couples. She'd been to office group lunches, but most of the conversation was of events she hadn't been to or about people she didn't know. A few of the people she worked with had invited her to parties at their homes, but when everyone else was a couple and she was a single, it wasn't much fun.

She wandered the mall for about half an hour, trying on a dress she would have loved and bought a few months ago. Now, realizing she had nowhere in particular to wear it, she put it back on the rack.

Heading back to her car she was close to tears. Wanting to get home as soon as she could she put the car in reverse and with only a cursory glance behind her backed out of the parking stall. Then came to a crashing halt as she backed into another car. It threw her forward and she dropped her head on the steering wheel and burst into tears.

She was vaguely aware of a man opening her car door and asking if she was all right. She nodded through her sobs.

"Are you sure you're not hurt?" he asked. "I honestly didn't see you backing up with all this rain."

"It's my fault," she said, "I was in such a hurry to get home, I didn't really look. And now look what's happened." She put her head down on the wheel again.

"Look, I don't think there's much damage done, it was mainly bumpers hitting together. Perhaps a dent in yours and a broken taillight in mine. But we need to exchange insurance information and it's too wet out here to do that. Why don't you pull back in your parking space and I'll find a spot, then we'll go in the Food Court in the mall and discuss this over a coffee."

She pulled back in the parking stall, grabbed her insurance papers and stuffed them in her purse. The man she'd hit found a spot only a few cars away and they walked silently into the mall.

Marianne dropped into a booth while he went and picked up two coffees. She started sobbing again, angry at herself for the mess she's made by not being careful. Once he'd returned with the coffees, he started talking about the weather and how it was to blame for the accident, asking her again if she was sure she wasn't hurt. Then he told her his name was Jim and asked her for her name, and asked if there was anything he could do to help her..

Marianne just looked at him and shook her head. Then she felt a tap on her arm and realized the elderly lady sitting next to her holding a red coat, was suggesting she listen to the nice man as he sounded like he wanted to help.

Realizing she was right, Marianne wiped her eyes and blew her nose, took a deep breath and for the first time got a good look at the man sitting across from her. He had deep brown eyes and the kindest face. She felt ashamed of her behavior and apologized.

"Jim…you did say Jim, didn't you?" At his nod she went on, "My name is Marianne."

Half an hour later they were still talking. He told her he was new in town and that she was the first woman outside of work he'd talked to in over a month. The insurance papers were on the table unread, and somewhere along the way he'd reached out and covered her hand with his.

Chapter 12

5:30 pm

Elly was pleased with her small interference in the food court. The young couple who appeared to have a problem were now holding hands and talking quietly.

It was time to go home. She usually caught the bus just outside the drug store so she headed in that direction. It had been a busy and eventful day and she was really tired. The comfortable chairs outside the drug store were now all empty as the mall was closing soon. Perhaps she'd rest a bit before catching her bus. She sat down, opened her purse and took out the lottery ticket to enjoy another look. She smiled as she noticed that she still hadn't circled the last winning number. Her eyes drifted closed momentarily. She couldn't remember feeling so tired.

6:00 pm

Buddy

Buddy came noisily down the hall with his cleaning cart. He hated this job and didn't care how much noise he made. It didn't make any difference anyway. The mall was closed, all the customers were gone and only a few staff were left closing up stores and securing things for the night.

He was tired and took his time. He'd already put in a full day's work. This was his second job.

Buddy's wife was expecting their third child, and with two others under five, she'd had to quit her job a few months ago. To pay the bills and keep from piling up debt, Buddy decided to take this second job as janitor at the mall. He worked construction during the day and then did a four hour shift from 6 to 10 pm at the mall. Some days he didn't even see his little ones.

As he came around the corner Buddy saw that not all the customers were gone. There was an old lady in a red coat sitting in a chair outside the drug store. She was sound asleep. He went over to wake her up and send her on her way, then noticed something odd about her. She didn't appear to be breathing. He pressed the pulse point in her neck and felt nothing.

"Holy Mother," he whispered. "She's dead."

He noticed a piece of paper in her hand and wondered if it had a name or number he could call, but when he looked at it he was shocked. It was a lottery ticket and it had five of the six numbers circled.

Well, he thought, *seeing that she'd won second prize must have been too much for her heart.*

He calculated quickly, realizing that second prize in the lottery must be somewhere between $30,000 and $100,000. The big prize was around $5 million.

"Well," he said under his breath, "this won't do you any good any more. But it will sure make a difference in my life."

He folded the lottery ticket carefully and put it in his shirt pocket under his work coveralls, then took out his phone and called mall security.

Made in the USA
Middletown, DE
26 April 2021

38127829R00027